RAINBOW MIST SCHOOL
CLASS GOLDEN FEATHER

My name is: Comet

My best friend is: My twin sister, Destiny

My favourite colour is: Purple

My favourite food is: Hay

I like to look after
my sister

RAINBOW MIST SCHOOL
CLASS GOLDEN FEATHER

My name is: Destiny

My best friend is: My twin brother, Comet

My favourite colour is: All the colours of the rainbow

My favourite food is: Grass

I like to do dares and
get into mischief!

Sue Bentley's books for children often include animals, fairies and wildlife. She lives in Northampton and enjoys reading, going to the cinema and watching the birds on the feeders outside her window. She loves horses, which she thinks are all completely magical. One of her favourite books is *Black Beauty*, which she must have read at least ten times. At school she was always getting told off for daydreaming, but she now knows that she was storing up ideas for when she became a writer. Sue has met and owned many animals, but the wild creatures in her life hold a special place in her heart.

Sue Bentley

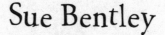

Riding Rescue

Illustrated by Angela Swan

PUFFIN

To Strawberry – pretty funster with attitude.

PUFFIN BOOKS

Published by the Penguin Group
Penguin Books Ltd, 80 Strand, London WC2R 0RL, England
Penguin Group (USA) Inc., 375 Hudson Street, New York, New York 10014, USA
Penguin Group (Canada), 90 Eglinton Avenue East, Suite 700, Toronto, Ontario, Canada M4P 2Y3
(a division of Pearson Penguin Canada Inc.)
Penguin Ireland, 25 St Stephen's Green, Dublin 2, Ireland (a division of Penguin Books Ltd)
Penguin Group (Australia), 250 Camberwell Road, Camberwell, Victoria 3124, Australia
(a division of Pearson Australia Group Pty Ltd)
Penguin Books India Pvt Ltd, 11 Community Centre, Panchsheel Park, New Delhi – 110 017, India
Penguin Group (NZ), 67 Apollo Drive, Rosedale, North Shore 0632, New Zealand
(a division of Pearson New Zealand Ltd)
Penguin Books (South Africa) (Pty) Ltd, 24 Sturdee Avenue, Rosebank,
Johannesburg 2196, South Africa

Penguin Books Ltd, Registered Offices: 80 Strand, London WC2R 0RL, England

puffinbooks.com

First published 2009
1

Text copyright © Sue Bentley, 2009
Illustrations copyright © Angela Swan, 2009
All rights reserved

The moral right of the author and illustrator has been asserted

Set in Bembo
Made and printed in England by Clays Ltd, St Ives plc

Except in the United States of America, this book is sold subject to the condition that it shall not, by way of trade or otherwise, be lent, re-sold, hired out, or otherwise circulated without the publisher's prior consent in any form of binding or cover other than that in which it is published and without a similar condition including this condition being imposed on the subsequent purchaser

British Library Cataloguing in Publication Data
A CIP catalogue record for this book is available from the British Library

ISBN: 978–0–141–32598–9

www.greenpenguin.co.uk

Mixed Sources
Product group from well-managed forests and other controlled sources
www.fsc.org Cert no. SA-COC-1592
© 1996 Forest Stewardship Council
FSC

Penguin Books is committed to a sustainable future for our business, our readers and our planet. The book in your hands is made from paper certified by the Forest Stewardship Council.

Prologue

Comet spread his gold-feathered wings as he glided above Rainbow Mist Island. Below him, the magic pony could see the tiny figures of pale horses with sparkling golden wings galloping towards a deep valley.

Lightning Horses – members of his own herd! Comet wondered if one of them could be Destiny, his long-lost twin sister.

Circling lower, he soared downwards to land and felt the velvety grass beneath his shining hooves. It felt good to be home.

As the magic pony galloped along, sunlight flashed on his cream-coloured coat and gold mane and tail. Through a gap in the rocks, he saw a waterfall gushing into a deep clear pool. Perhaps Destiny and the other Lightning Horses were making their way there to drink.

Checking his stride, Comet picked his way across big slabs of rock towards the tumbling water. Pastel-coloured ferns grew among a carpet of silver and gold flowers. Everything was wreathed in the fine multicoloured mist that gave Rainbow Mist Island its name.

Comet sensed a movement in some nearby birch trees and his lonely heart lifted with hope.

'Destiny!'

A pale cream horse with a wise expression stepped out. 'I am afraid she is not here. But it is good to see you again, my young friend,' he said in a deep musical whinny.

'Blaze!' Comet tried to hide his disappointment as he bent his head before the leader of the Lightning Herd. 'I hoped Destiny had come back.'

Blaze's gold eyes softened. 'I do not think she will return while she believes she is in trouble for losing our stone.'

The Stone of Power protected the herd from the dark horses who wanted to steal their power. It had been lost during their game of cloud-chasing. Comet had found the stone, but his twin sister had already fled.

'I can hardly bear to think of her being so far away and all alone,' Comet said sadly. 'Where can she be?'

'The stone will help us to find her.' Blaze stamped his front hoof on the grass and a gleaming fire-opal appeared, which shone with multicoloured light. 'Come closer. Look into the stone.'

As Comet did so, the stone grew in size and became brighter and brighter. An image appeared in its glittering depths. Comet saw Destiny cantering across a hillside in a world far away.

'I must go to her!' he cried.

There was a bright flash of violet light, and glittering rainbow mist swirled all around him. The young cream-coloured pony with gold-feathered wings and a gold mane and tail disappeared and in its place stood a sturdy Dartmoor pony, with a glossy bay coat, a paler sandy muzzle and a chocolate-brown mane and tail.

'Go now. Use this disguise and search for Destiny. Find her before the dark horses discover her,' Blaze neighed.

Comet nodded. 'I will bring her back safely!' he vowed.

A soft neigh rumbled from him and violet sparks glinted in his bay coat. Rainbow mist thickened and began wirling around him as it drew him in.

Chapter
ONE

Gina Carey smiled nervously up at the
young nurse who was about to remove
the plaster cast on her arm. 'Will it hurt?'
Gina asked her.

'You won't feel a thing. Promise!' the
nurse said reassuringly.

'Really?' Gina said doubtfully. She was
a real wimp when it came to anything to
do with doctors and hospitals.

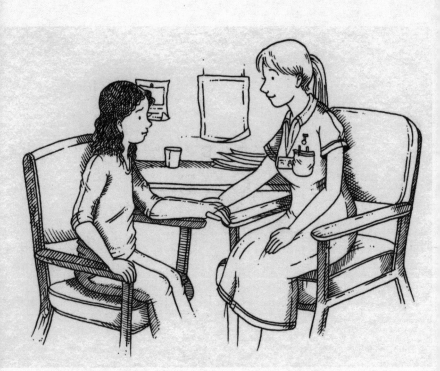

As the nurse got to work, there was a whiny, whirring noise. Mrs Carey stood nearby. She smiled at Gina. Moments later, the cast fell into pieces and the nurse removed it.

Gina grinned. 'Cool! It didn't even tickle!'

'Told you!' the nurse said, grinning. 'There, all done!'

'You'll be riding again in no time, love,' Mrs Carey said.

'I hope so.' Gina tried not to think about the riding accident in which she had broken her arm. She swallowed hard, determined not to get upset in front of the nurse.

Luckily, her mum was already gathering up her school bag and games kit. There was a queue of people waiting for treatment at the fracture clinic, so after a quick word of thanks to the nurse, they left and headed for the car park.

'That's school over with for a few weeks. Are you looking forward to summer camp with Katie and Lewis?' Mrs Carey asked as she drove home.

Katie and Lewis were Gina's best friends. They all went to Pony Club together.

'Mmm – yeah,' Gina murmured. She stared fixedly out of the side window for the rest of the short drive home.

The phone was ringing in the hall as they came through the front door and Gina hurried inside to answer it. It was Lewis, asking if she'd had her cast removed.

'Yep! Piece of cake!' Gina told him, missing out the bit about the butterflies in her tummy before it came off. 'My arm's all mended. It feels fine now.'

'Cool! So – are you packed and ready?' he asked. 'Dad's giving us all a lift to the coach park. It's going to be totally ace. Nothing to do all day but riding and pony stuff! I hope I don't get saddle sore!' he joked.

'Um . . . me too,' Gina said. 'See you

later. Bye.'

After Lewis rang off she stood in the hall, deep in thought. Who was she kidding? Since the accident she'd felt all wobbly at the mere thought of getting back on to a pony. She hadn't told anyone about this, hoping that she'd feel better by the time she went to summer camp.

Her mum was moving around the kitchen making lunch. Gina sighed heavily as she hovered in the doorway. She didn't hear her dad come out of his home office and almost jumped out of her skin when he touched her shoulder.

'You look a bit pale, Gina. Are you feeling OK?' Mr Carey asked.

'Yes. No. Not really. I . . . I . . .' To Gina's dismay, her eyes filled with tears and it all came pouring out. How she couldn't stop thinking about the accident and what had happened to River, her gentle grey pony. And how the very thought of riding sent her into a complete panic. 'I can't face going to camp! But I'll be letting Lewis and Katie down if I don't go,' she wailed.

'Oh, sweetheart!' Mrs Carey came over to give her a cuddle. 'You should have said earlier. You're still hurting after losing River. Katie and Lewis will understand.

I'll phone their parents right away and explain that you're giving camp a miss this time.'

'Thanks, Mum,' Gina gulped, feeling relieved.

Her mum went into the hall and returned a few minutes later. 'There. That's settled. No problem. Everyone was fine about it,' Mrs Carey said gently, smiling.

Gina's dad reached out to pat Gina's arm. 'Don't be too hard on yourself, love. It takes time to get over a shock. You'll ride again when you're ready.'

But I won't be riding River, Gina thought sadly. Her plucky little pony's injuries had been serious. She had gone to live in an animal park and would never be ridden again.

Gina forced herself to be brave as she tucked a strand of her dark hair behind her ears. She gave her mum and dad a watery smile, glad that they were being so nice and understanding.

'Now that you've time on your hands, how about coming with me to *Horseland*?' her mum suggested after a while. 'Angie will appreciate a bit of extra help.'

Angie Blackwell, a close family friend, had recently set up a horse and pony rescue centre. Gina's mum lent a hand whenever she could.

'OK. As long as I don't have to ride any of the ponies,' Gina said. She'd been itching to see how *Horseland* was coming along. The regular reports she'd been getting from her mum sounded great.

'You'll more likely be mucking out and

cleaning tack,' Mrs Carey said, gathering
the empty plates. 'Why don't you get
changed and I'll meet you at the car.'

'OK.' Gina took a deep breath. She was
feeling a bit better. 'See you later, Dad,'
she called, dashing upstairs to get her
jeans and wellies.

It was only a five-minute car ride to
the old farm. A big sign outside read:
HORSELAND. A SAFE HAVEN.
A NEW START.

Gina loved the message on the sign,
which offered hope to the rescued ponies.

They drove up the track to a large
stone farmhouse. Gina was impressed.
Angie had worked wonders with the
place. The old outbuildings had become
a stable block, tack room and storeroom.
Orange marigolds and blue pansies

glowed from the many tubs and window boxes.

They found Angie in her office, which overlooked the spacious yard. She was puzzling over a computer and looked up with a warm smile to greet Gina's mum. 'Hi again, Val. Nice to see you too, Gina. Come to see how we're doing, have you?'

Gina nodded. 'It's looking fantastic. Even better than I'd imagined.'

'It's been hard work. But it's a real labour of love.' Angie looked pleased. She had a friendly open face and clear bright blue eyes. Her shoulder-length fair hair was tied back in a pony tail. 'Why don't you have a wander around while I press-gang your mum into helping me sort out this database?'

'OK. See you both later.'

Gina went into the yard and sauntered towards the paddock, where some ponies were enjoying the sunshine. Whatever condition they had once been in, they all looked glossy and healthy now. She stepped on to the bottom bar of the ranch-style fence and folded her arms on the top. 'Hi, ponies. Who wants to come and say hello?' she invited.

One or two of them turned curious heads towards her.

A strange mist, twinkling with glittering rainbow sparkles, hung over the bottom of the paddock.

What a pretty trick of the sunlight, Gina thought. Just then a cute bay Dartmoor pony, with a chocolate-brown mane and tail and a sandy muzzle, stepped out of the mist and walked towards the fence.

'Hello, gorgeous.' Gina held out her hand so the bay pony could get her scent.

Twitching its ears forward inquisitively, the Dartmoor pony looked at her. 'Can you help me, please?' it asked in a velvety neigh.

Chapter
TWO

Gina snatched her hand back. Her eyes
widened as she almost fell backwards off
the fence in shock. Was this some kind
of a joke? She glanced round to see if
someone was hiding nearby and playing a
trick on her.

But her mum and Angie were still in
the office and the rest of the staff must be
inside the stables.

*I must be hearing things. Ponies can't talk
– not even rescued ones!* Gina shook her
head slowly. 'I wonder where you came
from,' she said aloud.

'I came from far away. I am Comet
of the Lightning Herd and I am here
looking for my twin sister,' the Dartmoor
pony said, looking at her with big deep
violet eyes.

'You . . . you really can talk!' Gina
gasped, still not actually believing this was
happening. 'How come?'

'All the Lightning Horses can talk,'
Comet explained. 'May I know your
name?'

He was looking at her steadily as if
he was expecting an answer. Gina found
herself stammering, 'G-Gina Carey. I'm . . .
h-here with my mum to help . . . with

the rescued horses. Mum's friend Angie
runs *Horseland*.'

'I am honoured to meet you, Gina.'
Comet dipped his head politely.

'Um . . . me too,' Gina said. She
remembered something he had said. 'Did
you say something about a twin sister? Is
she here too?'

'No. Destiny is hiding somewhere
nearby,' Comet said, his voice softening

with affection. 'She ran away after she lost the Stone of Power, when we were cloud-racing. The stone protects us from the dark horses who want to steal our magic. I found it and it is safe again, but Destiny does not know this. She thinks she is in terrible trouble, so she ran away to hide in your world.'

Gina was having trouble taking this in. It all sounded so strange, like something out of a fairy story. 'You say that you and your twin sister were cloud-racing – in the sky? But how can –'

Comet tossed his chocolate-brown mane and backed away from the fence. 'I will show you,' he whinnied gently.

Gina felt a strange warm tingling sensation flowing towards her fingertips as violet sparks glinted in Comet's glossy bay coat and another wash of shimmering rainbow mist swirled around him.

Gina narrowed her eyes, trying to see through the mist. Then her mouth fell open as she saw that the Dartmoor pony had gone, and in its place stood a magnificent cream-coloured pony with a noble arched neck and a flowing gold mane and tail. But even more amazing

were the gold-feathered wings that sprang from his shoulders.

'Oh!' Gina gasped, totally spellbound. She had never seen anything so beautiful in her entire life. 'Comet?'

'Yes, it is still me,' Comet said in a deep musical neigh.

But before Gina could get used to the dazzling sight of Comet in his true form, there was a final swoosh of the glittering rainbow mist and Comet reappeared as a strongly built Dartmoor pony.

'Wow!' Gina let out a long breath. 'That's an amazing disguise! Can Destiny use her magic to do that too?'

Comet nodded. 'But that will not help her if the dark horses discover her. They will see through her magic without the stone's protection. I must find her and

take her back safely to our home on
Rainbow Mist Island. Will you help me,
Gina?'

The magic pony's eyes twinkled
hopefully and Gina's soft heart melted as
she guessed he was missing his twin. 'Of
course I will. Wait until Mum and Angie
hear about this –'

'No! I am sorry, Gina, but you can tell
no one about me or what I have told
you!'

Gina hesitated, wishing that she could
share this amazing news. Her mum and
Angie would have been delighted to
think they had rescued a magic pony and
she was sure they would keep Comet's
secret.

'You must promise me,' Comet insisted
gently.

Gina came to a decision. She might not have been able to save River from getting hurt. But she would do anything she could to protect Comet and Destiny from their enemies.

'All right. Cross my heart. Your secret's safe with me.'

Comet's large intelligent eyes glowed softly like amethysts. 'Thank you, Gina.' He gave a soft blow and reached forward to nudge gently against her arm.

Gina stroked his velvety nose, which was a paler sandy colour than the rest of him. She breathed in his clean warm smell of grass and apples.

'Soon we will ride out and look for Destiny,' he breathed happily, his eyes closed in contentment.

'Um . . . yes. We will,' Gina said. To her dismay, she felt a familiar pang of anxiety at the thought of getting back into the saddle.

She felt proud that a magic pony had chosen her to be his special friend. There was no way she was going to let him down. Somehow she would find a way to keep her promise to him.

Chapter
THREE

'There you are, Gina!' Angie cried, striding towards the paddock. 'I've left your mum battling with the database. She's a proper computer whizz. Not like me! It looks like you've already made a friend.'

Gina smiled at Angie. 'I have! Comet's totally gorgeous, isn't he?' she said without thinking.

Angie looked surprised. 'Comet, eh? It suits him. We haven't come up with a name for this little bay yet, so I think we'll keep that one. He arrived in a truck a couple of days ago, along with some other ponies, but no one seemed to know much about him. Beats me how someone could just abandon a perfectly healthy young pony.'

'I know. I really hate people who do stuff like that,' Gina agreed with feeling. Of course, Comet hadn't actually been abandoned, but Gina knew that lots of ponies were. Thank goodness for places like *Horseland*.

Angie patted Comet's silky neck. 'Well, you two have certainly cosied up together. Comet didn't happen to tell you where he came from, did he, Gina?' she joked.

'As if!' Gina said, biting back a grin.
If only you knew! she thought.

Angie turned at the sound of an engine
and Gina saw a minibus trundling up the
track. 'It looks like the kids have arrived,'
Angie commented.

'Kids?' Gina said, puzzled.

'From a local children's centre. These
kids wouldn't usually get a chance to
meet ponies. But here they can interact
with them and even ride if they feel

confident enough. After what some of our ponies have been through, they find it less threatening to be around youngsters. It gets them back to feeling comfortable with adult riders.'

Gina thought this was a brilliant idea. She wondered what it would take to make *her* feel confident about riding Comet. She watched as the adult carers began helping some of the kids who were in specially adapted wheelchairs get off the bus as the others jumped off eagerly around them.

'Minky, especially, enjoys these sessions. That's him over there.' Angie pointed to a small black-and-white pony with a kindly expression, which one of her regular staff was now tacking up. She turned back to Gina. 'Comet seems a calm, sweet-natured pony. I think we'll see how he gets on with meeting the kids today. Would you like to help?'

'You bet!' Gina said eagerly. She had been perfectly willing to help muck out and clean tack, but this sounded much more fun. 'What do I have to do?'

'Bring Comet out and tether him in the yard. You'll find what you need in the tack room. OK?'

'Will do,' Gina said. 'Back in a tick, Comet!' she whispered. In a few moments she returned with a head collar and lead rope. 'I have to put this stuff on you. Is that OK?'

He nodded. 'I know of these straps that ponies wear in your world.'

Comet stood quietly while Gina fitted him with the head collar, led him into

the yard and tethered him beside Minky.
The small black-and-white pony nickered
and Comet gave an answering snort. Gina
smiled as the two ponies made friends.

Comet lifted his head and his chocolate
mane stirred in the breeze. 'This will be
fun!' he neighed.

Gina did a double take, amazed that
he'd just spoken to her. 'Hush!' she
warned him in a whisper. 'Someone
will hear you! You don't want to give

33

yourself away.'

'I have used my magic so that only you can hear me,' he told her, his deep violet eyes glinting. 'To anyone else I will look and sound like an ordinary pony.'

'Really? No problem then,' Gina whispered delightedly. Comet was so amazing. She wondered what else he could do.

Angie brought over a girl in a motorized wheelchair and a woman. Every centimetre of the wheelchair was covered with bright stickers of bands and singers.

'This is Felicity Norton and Jane, her carer. I'll leave them with you and Comet, Gina. OK?' she said with an encouraging smile. 'I'll be just across the yard. Call me if you need me.'

'No problem.' Gina felt a bit nervous, but hoped it didn't show. 'Hi, Felicity. I'm Gina Carey,' she said, smiling.

'Hi,' the girl replied. 'You can call me Fliss. Everyone does.' She looked about seven years old and had a delicate pale face with big hazel eyes. Her light brown hair was tied in bunches. She wore pink trainers and there was a sparkly star, in matching pink, on the front of her grey tracksuit.

Gina looked questioningly at Jane,
Fliss's carer.

The woman smiled. 'Don't mind me,
Gina. I'm just here to help Fliss get in and
out of the wheelchair. You two just carry
on. OK?'

'OK, fine,' Gina said. She turned back
to Fliss. 'This is Comet. He's a lovely
gentle pony.'

'He's blooming hu–uge!' Fliss turned to
Gina and looked her up and down. 'And
you don't look much older than me,' she
said bluntly. 'How come you've got a job
here?'

Gina grinned. 'I'm almost ten, but I
guess I look younger. I'm just helping
out. Angie knows that I've been around
ponies forever. I used to have my own
pony called River, but I haven't got her

any more.'

'Why not?' Fliss asked.

Gina bit her lip, wishing she hadn't mentioned her. 'It's a long story. Maybe I'll tell you some other time. How about you? Do you like ponies, Fliss?' she asked, quickly changing the subject.

'Dunno. Never met one.' Fliss shrugged her narrow shoulders.

'Never?' Gina couldn't imagine not having ponies in her life. 'Well, now's your chance,' she said encouragingly. 'You're going to love making friends with Comet!'

Fliss looked a bit nervous as she craned her neck to look up at Comet. 'What do I have to do?'

'Well – it's always best to come up to a pony from the side, rather than straight

on. He'll see you better that way and
you won't seem so scary to him. Talk to
Comet gently and then hold your hand
out flat, so he can get your scent. Do you
want to try that first and see how you get
on?'

'I can do that. It's not exactly rocket
science, is it?' Fliss scoffed, her eyes
twinkling cheekily. She pressed the
controls and her wheelchair trundled into
position.

Gina hid a smile. Fliss was a riot. She
wondered what Comet would make of
the outspoken little girl.

The magic pony's eyes softened as
he leaned down and snuffled Fliss's
outstretched palm. 'Hello, Fliss. Pleased to
meet you,' he neighed softly, but of course
Fliss heard only normal pony noises. He

then gently huffed a warm breath into her hair.

'Oh!' Fliss nearly jumped out of her skin. 'That *so* tickles!' she spluttered with delighted laughter. 'Why did he do that?'

'It's his way of being friendly,' Gina explained. 'Comet likes you.'

'Really? Cool! I like him too.' Her thin face brightening, she reached up slowly and tentatively stroked Comet's nose. 'Oh, it's lovely – all warm and soft, like velvet!'

Gina beamed as Fliss and Comet got to know each other. Fliss was soon confidently patting him and stroking his cheek. The meeting was a success!

'Maybe you'd like to sit on Comet's back another time?' she suggested. 'If that's OK with you?' she said, looking at Jane who stood nearby.

Fliss's carer nodded. 'No problem. I'll help her to get up on to the pony, but then she'll be fine.'

Fliss looked excited but apprehensive at the idea. 'Maybe. I dunno. It's an awful long way up. I'd have to think about it,' she said warily.

Angie strolled over. 'Well, you seem to be getting along well with Gina and Comet, Felicity. Would you like to meet some of our other ponies?'

'OK. But Comet's definitely my fave,' Fliss said, grinning proudly. 'He's totally awesome!'

'I couldn't agree more!' Gina said, smiling as Fliss, Jane and Angie crossed the yard. 'See you again soon!' she called.

'You bet!' Fliss shouted back, wheeling round to give her a double thumbs up.

'Bye, Comet. See you next time.'

Just then, there was a startled cry from one of the helpers.

Gina saw that a small boy was clinging on tight to Minky's back as the little black-and-white pony pranced about and pulled against its tether.

Angie was trying to calm the agitated

pony. 'Minky! Stand!' she said firmly.
'What's got into you?'

Gina frowned. Minky had seemed so
calm and friendly earlier. What could
be wrong? As the pony's eyes rolled and
his hindquarters tightened, she read
the tell-tale signs. 'Oh no!' she gasped.
'Minky's going to buck! That boy will be
thrown off!' Suddenly, she felt a tingling
sensation flowing down to the tips of her
fingers as big violet sparkles ignited in
Comet's bay coat and tiny rainbow flashes
of magical power rippled through his
chocolate-brown mane and tail.

Something very strange was about to
happen.

Chapter
FOUR

Gina watched in utter amazement as
Comet opened his mouth and breathed
out a long sparkly breath. A cloud
of shimmering multicoloured glitter
whooshed across the yard towards Minky.
Gina looked around to see if anyone else
could see the magical rainbow mist, but it
seemed visible only to her.

The glittering particles whirled around

the black-and-white pony for a few seconds, making it look as if Minky stood in the centre of a snow-dome. Then the sparkles faded away into rainbow dust and disappeared, along with every last violet spark.

The panic left the little pony's eyes and they grew calm again. Minky stood quietly as Angie and one of the carers helped the boy get down from the pony and back into his wheelchair.

Gina could see little tremors flickering over the pony's black-and-white coat and he was twitching his tail in distress. She frowned. 'There's still something wrong with him.'

Comet thought so too. Swivelling his ears, he whickered to Minky. The little pony turned his head. Wrinkling his

lips, he nickered back.

Comet listened closely and then neighed softly to Gina. 'Minky has told me that something is digging into his back and hurting him.'

'Oh, the poor thing. No wonder he was playing up,' Gina said.

She hurried straight over to Angie who

looked very embarrassed. 'Oh dear. I'm
so sorry you've had a scare, Tommy,' she
apologized to the boy. 'Minky's usually so
steady and reliable. I don't know what got
into him today.'

Tommy grinned up at her, his face
flushed. 'I'm OK! It was almost like being
in a rodeo!' he said, looking none the
worse for his fright.

'I'm afraid that's not the point, though,
Tommy,' said the carer, a tall young man
named Bill. 'How do we know that this
won't happen again?'

'Well –' Angie began.

'Excuse me, but I've got an idea about
what happened,' Gina interrupted politely.
'Do you mind if I look at Minky's saddle?'

Angie raised her eyebrows in surprise.
'Go ahead,' she said, looking puzzled.

Gina loosened the girth and removed Minky's saddle. She ran her fingers under it, where they immediately snagged on a small prickly seedhead. 'Just as I thought!' She extracted the burr and showed it to Angie. 'This was digging into Minky's back!'

'So that's why he shied!' Angie patted Minky's cheek. 'Poor boy. You were trying to tell us you were in pain.' She looked at

Gina. 'Thanks, love. It was clever of you to work that out,' she praised warmly.

Gina smiled. 'It wasn't that hard,' she said modestly.

She wished she could tell Angie that it was Comet who deserved all the credit, but she would never reveal his secret.

With the mystery solved, Gina left Angie smoothing things over with Tommy and the carer. She patted Comet and stroked his thick mane. 'Well done, Comet,' she whispered, looking at him adoringly. 'You were brilliant!'

The magic pony twitched his tail. 'I am glad that I could help.'

Gina felt a rush of affection for her magical friend. She decided that he deserved a treat. 'I'll be right back!' she told him, dashing off towards the stable kitchen in search of an especially juicy, crunchy apple.

'So you enjoyed your first visit to *Horseland*?' Mrs Carey asked later as they drove home.

'It was totally brilliant. The rescued ponies are lovely,' Gina enthused. 'It's hard to believe that some of them were once neglected. The ones I met all look in great condition. Minky, the little black-and-white pony, is really cute. And there's Dancer, she's a roan-coloured Welsh pony. And Porter is stunning. He's an ex-showjumper. And then there's Comet, the bay Dartmoor pony. He's absolutely gorgeous, the best of all! And –'

'Whoa! Slow down a bit,' her mum said, laughing. 'I can't keep up!'

Gina grinned. 'Sorry. I got a bit carried away. It's a fantastic place. Can I go over there again tomorrow? Angie says I'm welcome any time.'

'Course you can. Angie was very impressed with you. She told me what happened with Minky. You helped her with what could have been a very difficult situation. Well done, love. I'm very proud of you.'

Gina blushed. 'Oh, it wasn't much.'

'Well, I'm very impressed,' her mum said firmly. 'And I can see that you've totally fallen in love with that bay. What's his name again?'

'Comet,' Gina said. 'He's pretty special.'

'He certainly seems to have worked some kind of magic on you.'

'What ... what do you mean?' Gina

asked nervously. Had her mum heard
her talking to the magic pony? *Please tell
me I haven't given away Comet's secret*, she
thought, her heart thumping.

Mrs Carey smiled. 'I just meant that
you're like a different girl. You were pretty

wound up at lunch. I was surprised that you even agreed to come to *Horseland*.'

Gina breathed a sigh of relief. 'I'm glad I did, or I wouldn't have met Comet. I love him to bits. And so does Fliss. She's a little girl I met today. Angie let me introduce her to Comet,' she said proudly. 'Fliss was quite nervous at first, but then she calmed down. I reckon I might get her to try riding Comet.'

'Well, that would be lovely – quite something,' her mum said. 'Oh no, wait a minute. I've just remembered. I have to take the car to the garage tomorrow morning, so I can't give you a lift.'

'That's OK. I can cycle over,' Gina said at once.

Her mum's eyes widened in shock. 'Since when did you offer to cycle anywhere? You really *are* keen to be around those rescued ponies, aren't you? I don't blame you. It's a great feeling when you see the poor things beginning to get their confidence back and learning to trust people again.'

Gina nodded. She couldn't agree more. 'If only I could get *my* confidence back to start riding again,' she murmured wistfully, thinking of helping Comet look for Destiny.

Her mum gave her a knowing grin. 'Trust me, love. Someone as pony-mad as you won't be able to resist getting back into the saddle for very much longer!'

Gina smiled and her spirits lifted a little as she hoped her mum was right.

Chapter
FIVE

Gina woke up the next morning to find
the sun shining through her bedroom
curtains. Birdsong twittered from the
nearby trees, but it was so early that she
couldn't hear any cars going past on the
road outside.

She was longing to see Comet again, if
only to prove that yesterday hadn't been
just an incredible dream. Throwing back

the duvet, she shot out of bed and threw on her shorts and T-shirt. After a hurried gulp of fruit juice in the kitchen, she left a note for her mum and dad to tell them where she'd gone, grabbed her bike and set out for *Horseland*.

It had been ages since Gina had ridden her bike and she was puffing hard by the time she reached the top of the hill above the old farm. She rested her aching leg muscles when she coasted down the slope

on the other side and then turned into *Horseland*'s entrance.

Morning mist still covered the grass in the empty paddock and Gina guessed that all the ponies were still shut up safely in the stable. There was no sign of Angie or any of her staff, so opening the door she slipped inside.

Comet was looking over his stall and spotted her immediately. He gave a neigh of welcome. 'Greetings, Gina!'

'Hi, Comet!' Gina threw her arms round the magic pony's silky neck and pressed her cheek against his warm skin. 'I missed you, so I cycled over here the moment I got up.'

'Thank you for coming here this early,' Comet snorted. There was a little flurry of sparks and the door of his stall opened.

He stepped out to stand beside her. 'Now we have time to go out looking for Destiny. Please climb on to my back.'

Gina froze and her mouth dried. Maybe if she just climbed straight up on to Comet's back, she'd feel OK.

But her legs trembled as she stepped on to the mounting block. *I have to do this*, she told herself. With a super-human effort, she forced herself to swing her right leg up and over. Closing her eyes and fighting a wave of panic, she took a firm hold of his mane.

'R-ready,' she murmured shakily.

Comet didn't move. His ears flattened and he turned to look at her. 'Is something wrong, Gina? You do not seem happy to ride me.'

Gina swallowed and tears burned her

eyes. 'I do want to, more than anything!
But . . . I . . . j–just can't. Not yet!'
She scrambled off his back on to the
mounting block. Once on the ground,
she stood with her head down and her
arms hanging by her sides. 'I'm so sorry,
Comet. I've let you down! I wouldn't
blame you if you hated me! You should

find someone else to help you, someone
who isn't useless!' she burst out.

She whirled and ran into the stable
yard. Tears of humiliation blinded her. She
had failed Comet. There was no way she
could keep her promise to help him find
Destiny.

Suddenly, Comet was walking beside
her, his shining hooves making no sound
on the ground.

'Please stop, Gina,' he neighed softly,
turning to look at her with kind eyes.
'You must tell me everything.'

Gina nodded wretchedly. She took a
deep breath and told her magical friend
everything. 'I . . . I had a bad accident a
few months ago. I was in a field, riding
my pony, River, when a car backfired
nearby and scared her. River reared up

and I fell off and broke my arm. She bolted and caught her foot in a rabbit hole and hurt herself really badly. River almost had to be –' Gina stopped for a moment, unable to say the awful words. 'But she got well enough to go and live in an animal park. I lost my lovely pony. And I've been really scared to ride since then.'

Comet nodded slowly and his mane fell forward. 'That was a horrible thing to happen. It is very sad to lose a dear friend. On Rainbow Mist Island we have a saying: "No one is ever far away when they are in our memories."'

Gina laid her face against his warm cheek and was surprised to feel her sadness easing a little. 'That's true. I think about River every day and Mum says we

can go and visit her sometime. I know
she would want me to ride again, but
the thought of it still scares me stiff,' she
admitted, hanging her head.

Comet was silent for a moment. 'I have
an idea,' he neighed at last.

'Really?' Gina looked up into the
magic pony's beautiful eyes, which
glowed with affection and understanding.

'Are you going to use your magic to make me forget about what happened and stop me being afraid?' she asked hopefully.

'No, Gina. That would not be right. Our memories are part of who we are. You must find a way to be strong. I will not always be here to solve problems for you.'

Gina felt a pang as she realized that one day her friend must leave and return to his own world with his twin sister. But she couldn't bear to think of that right now.

'Thank you for being so kind, Comet. You're the best friend ever,' she said, holding out her hands.

Comet gently pushed his nose into her cupped palms. She felt his warm breath

on her fingers as they shared a moment
of closeness she knew she would treasure
always.

'Are you going to look for Destiny
now?' she asked eventually.

Comet nodded, a gleam of
determination in his eyes. 'Yes. And you
are going to help me!'

'But . . . but . . . how can I?' Gina's heart
missed a beat. Was he going to insist that
she rode him after all?

Chapter
SIX

Gina gasped as she felt a tingling
sensation flow right down to the ends of
her fingertips. Large violet sparks glowed
in the magic pony's bay coat and a thick
mist flowed around them, shimmering
and glowing with all the colours of the
rainbow.

She felt something soft and springy
beneath her feet and looked down to see

that she and Comet were standing on a small white fluffy cloud.

'Hold tight, Gina!' Comet instructed.

Gina wrapped one hand in his thick chocolate mane. She felt a surge of excitement as they rose into the air and floated across the fields. Suddenly, they shot forward on the cloud, whizzing

across hills and valleys and zooming along above forests and woods.

Two surprised-looking wood pigeons fluttered out of a tree as they flew past. A grey squirrel chattered and dived for cover.

'Wow! This is brilliant!' Gina exclaimed as they raced along at the speed of light. It was wonderful to be pressed up close against Comet's warm, strong shoulder and feel his glittery magic enfolding her. She felt safe and secure beside him on the pillowy cloud, however high they floated in the air.

They descended once to check out some ponies in a field, but none of them were Destiny. For the rest of their trip, Gina and Comet saw no other ponies.

As Comet's ears flattened with

disappointment, Gina stroked his satiny neck. 'We'll find her. We'll keep on looking until we do,' she promised. 'You never know, she might already have come past this way.'

'No, she has not, Gina. Or she would have left a trail,' Comet told her.

Gina was intrigued. 'What sort of trail?'

'A line of softly glowing hoof-prints. Not many people in your world can see them.'

'Will I be able to?' Gina asked.

Comet nodded. 'Yes, if you are riding me or we are very close.' He looked up at the sky, where the sun was now above the trees. 'We must return to *Horseland* – they will be wondering where you are.'

Gina clung on tight to his mane as the cloud whooshed back through the clear

morning air above the tree-tops.
A patchwork of fields rushed past below
them, along with miniature villages and
roads with toy-town cars and houses. In
no time at all they were hovering over
the familiar farmhouse and stable yard.

There was a final violet flash and a
burst of rainbow sparkles and Gina found
herself back on solid ground, standing
inside the stable in front of Comet's stall.
It wasn't a moment too soon.

Angie Blackwell came in, wheeling a
barrow. 'So it's your bike outside! That
solves the mystery,' she said with a broad
grin. 'You're an early bird this morning.'

Gina grinned. 'I know. I just couldn't
keep away.'

'Come to see Comet again, have you?
That's so sweet.' Angie looked delighted.

'You certainly seem to have a way
with him. I had a phone call from the
children's centre yesterday afternoon
to say that the kids had a great time.
Especially Felicity. Apparently, she's been
raving about you and Comet. She's asked
if they can all visit again today.'

'Isn't that great?' Gina was delighted that Fliss had enjoyed herself so much. Helping someone discover a love for ponies was the best feeling in the world.

'Yes, it is,' Angie agreed. 'I love to see the kids and ponies together. But with an extra visit, it means we have rather a frantic day. There's a new pony arriving later. By all accounts it's in rather a bad state, so I'd prefer any visitors to be out of the way when it arrives.'

'Oh, what a shame,' Gina said, already worried for the poor pony.

'Do you know if your mum's planning on coming over?' Angie asked. 'We really could do with some extra help today.'

'She has to take the car into the garage this morning – that's why I cycled over earlier. Maybe you could phone her and ask if she's coming here later?' Gina suggested. 'But I can stay and help. What do you want me to do?'

'You're a star. Thanks, Gina. Could you turn out the ponies into the paddock for me and then help with mucking out?'

'No problem!' Gina said, already crossing the stable.

She led Minky and Dancer out first, watching as the little black-and-white pony and the sturdy roan kicked up their heels and cantered to the bottom of the field. She then came back for Porter, the beautiful ex-showjumper, before finally leading Comet out.

'I'll see you later,' she said to him as she closed the paddock gate. 'I loved floating on that cloud with you. It was fun, wasn't it?' she said fondly.

The magic pony's deep violet eyes
gleamed affectionately. 'Yes, it was. It
reminded me of cloud-racing with
Destiny.'

Gina noticed a flicker of sadness cross
his face. 'We'll go out looking again really
soon.'

Comet brightened. 'Thank you, Gina.'
He turned and trotted towards Minky,
who was already cropping the sweet grass.

*

Gina thought about Comet's kindness to her as she finished mucking out. 'He's the best friend anyone could have,' she said to herself.

She was determined to ride him properly the next time they went out searching for Destiny. Comet had been really good about them using the cloud, but it would be much quicker and they could do a better ground search if she rode him. Besides, she owed it to her special friend.

Gina was putting away the fork and skip when Angie called across the yard to say that hot chocolate and food were ready in the farmhouse.

'I've spoken to your mum and she's popping over later. She also said it looked as if you'd missed breakfast. So you're to get yourself over here, young lady. Pronto!' Angie ordered, smiling.

'Yes, ma-am!' Gina called back, grinning.

Her tummy was rumbling like a freight train and she realized she was starving. She pushed a strand of hair off her sweaty face and went to wash her hands. In the farmhouse kitchen, Angie and a couple of her staff were seated at a huge wooden table, tucking into huge plates of cooked breakfast. Gina joined them. Her

toasted bacon sandwiches and mug of hot chocolate were delicious.

'Hot chocolate in the middle of summer?' Angie teased with a grin.

'Any time of year is hot chocolate time!' Gina insisted, draining her mug.

The second she finished eating, she excused herself and went back outside to Comet. The minibus had just pulled up in the yard and the carers and kids were getting out.

'Fliss is first off the bus,' Gina told Comet. 'She must be really keen to see you again.'

'I am glad to see her too!' Comet neighed, and twitched his tail as Fliss whirred towards him in her colourful wheelchair. Her carer, Jane, walked beside her.

'Hiya, Gina! Hiya, Comet!' Fliss wore a lemon tracksuit today and there were purple bangles on her thin wrists.

'Hello, Gina,' said Jane, smiling.

Gina greeted them warmly. 'Hi, Jane. Hi, Fliss. Good to see you again.' She thought the little girl looked even paler than the previous day. There were dark shadows beneath her eyes. But the moment she saw Comet, Fliss's face lit up. She reached up to pat his cheek, and Comet bent his head so Fliss could put her arms round his neck and give him a hug.

'You remember me, don't you, boy?' Fliss crooned, giving him a big wet kiss on his nose. She glanced at Gina, a look of determination on her small pinched face. 'OK. I've made my mind up! I want to ride him now – right now!'

Gina looked at Jane, who nodded. 'No problem. I'll help.'

Looking back at Fliss, Gina grinned. 'You're on!'

Chapter SEVEN

'Feel OK up there?' Gina asked Fliss. 'Tell me if you want Comet to stop, so you can have a rest, won't you?'

'No chance!' Fliss cried.

Gina led Comet slowly round the yard, with Fliss sitting in the bulky western-style saddle, which supported her small frame better than an English one.

'I'm *so* loving this!' Fliss said, beaming

from ear to ear as she clung tightly to the pommel at the front of the saddle. 'I'm actually riding a pony! Yay!'

Comet was enjoying himself too. He moved at a smooth gentle pace and kept his head up high, so the little girl wouldn't fall if she slipped forward. But nothing happened and Fliss rode around the yard with a big grin on her face. 'Look at me!' she called, waving to everyone she passed.

After the session, Jane helped Fliss dismount and get back in her wheelchair. As she settled down, Fliss seemed to sink with tiredness. But she still insisted on giving Comet a goodbye hug before she left. 'See you again soon, Comet!' she said in a faint voice. 'Bye, Gina. And thanks a bunch. I had a mega-fab time.'

'Me too. I'm glad you enjoyed it,' Gina said, a bit worried that Fliss seemed so tired after such a short ride. She stood beside Comet, waving as the minibus drove away.

Angie came over as Gina was unbuckling Comet's saddle. 'I'm glad Fliss had fun. She's got some good memories to take with her into hospital.'

'Hospital?' Gina exclaimed.

Angie nodded. 'Jane told me she has to have regular treatment for her condition.

Apparently Fliss is used to it, but she gets very fed up with having to stay in hospital for a week at a time.'

'Oh, what a shame,' Gina said sympathetically. That explained why Fliss had looked unwell, although she had been trying to hide it.

'Fliss is a brave girl. I like her,' Comet neighed as she removed his bridle.

'Me too,' Gina agreed. 'I hope she'll be OK.' She wished she could do something to help. Maybe she'd ask her mum if they could visit her in hospital.

She unbuckled the western-style saddle and put it away before coming out of the tack room. 'Time for some yummy oats for you,' she said to Comet.

Just then a jeep with a trailer pulled into the yard. Shrill squeals and neighs came from inside. There was a clang of hooves against the metal sides.

'That new pony doesn't sound good,' Gina said. She was dying to go and peer over the trailer's back door and see what was making such a noise. 'Do you mind waiting for your oats for a minute?' she asked Comet.

Comet shook his head, his ears swivelling towards the trailer. 'I would like to wait here and see the new pony too.'

Gina watched anxiously as Angie and the jeep's driver unbolted and then let down the trailer's ramp. Cowering inside, her eyes rolling in fear, was the thinnest pony Gina had ever seen. The little mare was a lovely deep chestnut colour, with a flaxen mane and tail and four white socks. Her mane and tail were tangled and her

coat and feet were caked in mud.

'Oh, the poor thing,' Gina said breathlessly. 'You can see all her ribs. She's going to need lots of feeding up.'

The rescued pony whinnied and kicked out again, pulling against the frayed rope that tethered her, her ears twitching madly. Gina was frightened she'd hurt herself against the trailer's sides.

Comet neighed softly and the other pony froze in shock. Pricking up her ears, she turned her head towards Comet and listened to him with surprise. After a moment, she gave a rather nervous nicker of reply.

Comet nodded and then snorted reassuringly. 'She says her name is Willow,' he told Gina. 'She doesn't trust humans. She thinks they are all mean and cruel.'

'Oh, that's awful!' Gina's soft heart went out to Willow, who was now shivering and trembling with fear.

Gina immediately wanted to show the pretty chestnut pony that not all humans were horrible. But how did you persuade such a scared pony that you didn't mean her any harm?

Comet neighed again and Willow listened more calmly. This time, when the magic pony finished, Willow turned to

look at Gina. Her large dark eyes were
calmer now and her ears were pricking
forward in curiosity.

Gina couldn't believe the change in the
little chestnut. 'What did you say to her?'
she whispered to Comet.

'She asked who you were. I told her
that you are a kind person, who she
can trust.' His violet eyes softened.

'Willow needs you, Gina.'

Gina gulped as Comet's words sank deeply into her. It seemed like an impossible task, but she knew that she had to help this little chestnut mare. Looking up at Comet, she gave him a smile of total trust.

Angie took charge. 'Right. Stand back, everyone. Time to get this pony into a nice clean stable.' She moved towards the ramp and had barely put her foot on the bottom of it when Willow reared up in alarm and the frayed rope she was tied with snapped.

'Oh no! Steady there, girl,' Angie said softly. 'No one's going to hurt you.'

But Willow wasn't listening. She snorted, squealed and stamped and tried to wheel round in the small space.

'OK. I get the message,' Angie said, backing away and stepping down. She drew a hand through her fair hair. 'Poor little thing. She's terrified. We need to get her out of there before she really hurts herself. But I can't see her letting anyone near her.'

Gina found herself walking over to the trailer. 'She'll let me,' she said confidently. 'I'll try, Angie.'

Angie shook her head. 'No, Gina. Absolutely not. It's much too dangerous . . .'

Chapter
EIGHT

Gina felt a stir of dismay. She looked at
the terrified chestnut pony, cowering in
the corner of the trailer and knew she
couldn't take no for an answer.

'Ple–ase, Angie. I'll be very careful,' she
said in her most persuasive voice.

Angie frowned doubtfully. 'I still don't
think it's a good idea –'

'You can watch me the whole time!'

Gina rushed on. 'And I promise I won't go too close, until you tell me it's safe. Please, Angie,' she said again. 'I have to do this!'

'This means a lot to you, doesn't it?'

'Yes, it does.'

Angie nodded slowly. 'Well, all right. But go very slowly and don't take your eyes off her. And high-tail it backwards right away if I tell you to. OK?'

'Deal,' Gina agreed.

Despite her earlier confidence, her tummy clenched with nerves as she went over to stand beside Angie and looked up the ramp.

'Hello, girl,' she said softly. 'Don't be scared. I'm Gina and I want to be your friend. You're going to love it here.' She kept her voice low. 'This is a great place and everyone wants to make you better. Just give us a chance . . .'

Willow stood still, watching with wide eyes.

'So far, so good,' Angie said approvingly. 'You're doing fine.'

Some instinct told Gina not to move up the ramp. 'That's good. See? I'm not mean or scary,' she said gently. 'I'm just going to stand here.'

Willow twitched her ears, as if to say, *Why are you waiting there?* Ducking her head, she lifted one dainty front leg. She took a small step forward. Twitching her matted tail, she took another step.

Now she had her front hooves on the ramp. She stood there calmly, a bit surprised at herself and then looked up at Gina expectantly.

'Oh, so now you want me to show you your smart new stable, huh?' Gina waited patiently as Willow came slowly down the ramp. Gina resisted the urge to reach out, and stood with her hands behind her back.

Willow came close and sniffed her T-shirt and jeans, getting used to her scent.

After a few moments, Gina spoke gently again. 'Ready now? Come on, then.' She crossed her fingers, slowly turned and took a few steps.

Willow stepped off the ramp and followed her.

Gina stopped, reached smoothly behind her and took hold of the broken rope. 'Here we go. Brave girl. You did really well,' she crooned as she led the little mare into the stable, put her in her stall and bolted the door.

'Good job, Gina,' Angie congratulated Gina as she came back into the yard. 'That was very impressive. You've got a real instinct for this work. How do you fancy working with Willow? It will be a slow process and you'll need a lot of patience. But she seems to trust you and that's a big first step for a pony that's been treated so badly. What do you say?'

'I say yes. Yes, please!' Gina said, proud that Angie trusted her with such an important job. 'Wait until I tell Com— I mean, er . . . Mum,' she corrected herself quickly. 'She won't believe it!'

She hurried over to where Comet was waiting and told him the news. 'Isn't that fantastic? But I couldn't have done it without your help.'

Comet nudged her arm affectionately. 'I did not do very much. You helped Willow overcome her fear by staying calm and letting her come to you.'

'Yeah, I guess I did!' Gina said. 'It was really weird. I completely forgot to be nervous or scared, because I was too busy thinking about Willow.'

Comet nodded wisely. 'Sometimes we are braver than we think we are.'

Over the next few days, Gina arrived early every morning at *Horseland*. She helped with mucking out stables, leading out and exercising the ponies, cleaning tack and grooming. And there were always visitors to show round, and new ponies and horses arriving. She was making good progress with Willow.

The little chestnut mare now pricked her ears and stood calmly when Gina approached her stall.

The weekend dawned bright and clear when Gina's mum dropped her at *Horseland* on her way to the shops. 'Have fun. And say hi to Comet for me!'

'I will. Thanks for the lift!' Gina waved as her mum drove away.

She went straight into the stable to see Comet before she started work, as she always did. Two friendly whinnies rang out and Gina did a double take.

'Did you hear that, Comet? Willow just said hello to me too!'

Gina slowly reached up to stroke the chestnut mare's nose. Willow flicked her ears, but didn't shy away. She gave a long soft contented blow, as if to say 'this place isn't too scary after all'.

'She's so pretty,' Gina said as she looked into the mare's big dark eyes. 'I think Willow and I are going to become good friends.' Gina beamed at Comet.

Comet nodded. His violet eyes gleamed with satisfaction.

Later, Gina was brushing Comet's deep bay coat until it gleamed, when she heard Angie talking to one of the staff inside the tack room. '. . . such a shame. She was doing so well, until she found out she has to stay in hospital longer. The doctor said she needs something to cheer her up.'

'They're talking about Fliss!' Gina realized with a stab of guilt. She remembered that she had planned to visit the sick girl but, with Willow arriving, the thought had gone right out of her mind. She had an idea. 'Comet! How about if we . . .'

The magic pony listened hard as she explained. 'It is a good plan,' he said. 'Lead me to the bush at the bottom of the paddock, Gina.'

Gina did so. All she could think about was poor lonely unhappy Fliss. Well, she was about to get one huge surprise.

'Ready? Climb on to my back, Gina,' Comet neighed, his eyes twinkling expectantly.

Gina took a deep breath. *I know I can do this*, she silently told herself. Fliss needed her and Comet. Before her courage failed her again, Gina climbed up, sat astride Comet and wrapped her hands in his mane. 'Let's go!' she urged determinedly, kicking him on.

A familiar prickling sensation flowed down her fingers as violet sparks ignited in Comet's bay coat and tiny misty rainbows glimmered around him. He leapt forward and sped away.

Comet gave a neigh of triumph. 'Well done, Gina. You are riding again!'

'Oh my goodness. So I am!' Gina

gasped in amazement. 'Wow! I really am! And I'm not a bit scared!' She could hardly believe it. Riding the magic pony felt like the most natural thing in the world.

Comet's tail streamed out behind him as he galloped along invisibly. 'You were too busy thinking about Fliss to feel scared. Just like with Willow. You did not need magic. Your own kindness has cured you!'

Gina realized that he was right. She could feel proud of herself for conquering her fear. And her reward was riding the most amazing pony in the universe!

Chapter
NINE

A surge of happiness glowed through
Gina from head to toe. She felt as if she
was filled with fizzy lemonade. Comet
was wonderful to ride, so fast and smooth.
His warm magic made her feel safe,
no matter how swiftly he weaved past
obstacles and dodged past anything in
their way.

She wanted to go on riding her

magical friend forever, and never stop!

Crouching over, Gina moved expertly in time to his powerful strides. She realized how much she had missed riding and knew that River would be glad she had worked through her fear. She promised herself that she'd go to visit the little grey pony in the animal park and tell her all about Comet.

'Wow! I love this so much! Go, Comet, go!' she cried.

As the hospital came in sight, Comet leapt into the air and his hooves carried them upwards and over it in a mighty leap. A sprinkle of rainbow dust rained down and, in the centre of it, Gina saw a small pale little girl sitting in bed in a room next to the car park.

'There's Fliss!' she said, pointing.

'I see her.' Comet landed in the car park, next to some bushes. Suddenly, he stopped and looked down at the ground.

Gina peered over his shoulder to see what he was looking at. Her eyes widened.

Stretching away across the hospital car park was a faint line of softly glowing, violet hoof-prints.

'Destiny has been here!' Comet told her.

Gina gasped. Did that mean he was leaving right now to go after his twin? 'Is she somewhere nearby?' she asked anxiously.

'No, the trail is cold. But now I know that Destiny came this way. When I am closer to her, I will hear her hoof-beats.'

'Will I be able to hear them?' Gina asked.

'Yes, if we are together. But other humans will not hear them. And I may have to leave suddenly, without saying goodbye, to catch up with Destiny,' he said seriously.

Gina bit back a new surge of dismay. 'Couldn't you and Destiny stay at

Horseland; then we could all be friends?'
she asked hopefully in a wobbly voice.

Comet shook his head. 'I am afraid
that is not possible. We must return to
Rainbow Mist Island and our family.
I hope you understand, Gina?'

Gina nodded sadly. She swallowed

hard and tried not to think about Comet leaving.

'Let's go and see Fliss now,' she suggested, changing the subject.

She dismounted and they walked down a path at the side of the hospital building. Fliss lay on a bed in her room. She looked very tired and pale.

The window was open and Gina tapped on it to get her attention.

Fliss frowned. As she turned and saw them, she did a double take. A huge smile spread over her face. 'Comet? Gina? What are you doing here?'

'We came to see you,' Gina said, smiling back. She opened the window a bit more, so that Comet could put his head inside the room.

Fliss laughed with delight. 'Way to go,

Comet! I bet that's the first time a pony's been inside this hospital.' She looked at Gina, puzzled. 'Did you get here in a horsebox or something?'

'Um . . . yeah, kind of,' Gina said evasively, only just realizing that she hadn't thought about explanations. 'But I . . . er, borrowed Comet without Angie knowing, so don't tell anyone. Or I'll be in big trouble. OK?'

'Cross my heart!' Fliss exclaimed. 'I can't believe this. It's mega-cool!'

'So – how are you?' Gina asked.

Fliss's cheeks were flushed as pink as her tracksuit. 'I *was* dead bored. But I'm not now. Tell me what's happening at *Horseland* and don't miss anything out!'

'Well, a new pony arrived. She's called Willow. You're going to love her . . .'

*

Gina held tight as Comet galloped back towards *Horseland*. They swept along past houses, shops and roads until they came to open countryside. Moments later, the old farmhouse came into view.

'That was brilliant, Comet. We really

cheered Fliss up, didn't we?'

Comet snorted agreement. With a final surge and a sprinkle of violet glitter, he bounded into the paddock. Minky, Dancer and Porter were already in there, nibbling the sweet grass and enjoying the sunshine.

And so was a little chestnut mare with a flaxen mane and tail and four white socks.

'Willow!' Gina cried.

She was delighted to see the little mare with the other ponies. Even after a few days the change in Willow was amazing. She had begun to put on weight and her coat was starting to shine. When Willow saw Gina and Comet, she trotted over to the fence.

Gina dismounted and she and Comet

walked over to her. Willow huffed out
a warm breath and rubbed her chestnut
nose against his silky neck. Comet gently
nibbled her mane.

Gina smiled at them. They were so
sweet.

She looked at the stables, imagining all
the ponies to come who would need her
help. And she knew what she wanted to
do for the rest of her life.

As she smiled at Comet, she felt like
the luckiest girl in the world.

It was unusually quiet, with no one
around. Gina guessed they were all in the
farmhouse having a tea break. Suddenly,
she heard a sound she'd been hoping for
and dreading at the same time.

The hollow sound of galloping hooves
overhead.

She froze. Destiny was here! There was no mistake.

Comet flicked his tail and raced down to the bottom of the paddock. Gina ran after him and reached him just as there was a bright flash and rainbow mist swirled around him.

In the middle of it Comet stood there in his true form, a dark bay Dartmoor pony no longer. Sunshine gleamed on his noble arched neck, cream coat and flowing golden mane and tail. Magnificent wings, covered with gold feathers, spread upwards from his shoulder.

'Comet!' Gina gasped. She had almost forgotten how beautiful he was. 'Are ... are you leaving right now?'

His glowing violet eyes softened, and sadness flickered across them for a moment. 'I must. If I am to catch Destiny and take her home safely.'

Gina's eyes stung with tears. She swallowed hard as she knew she must find the courage to let her friend go. She ran forward, threw her arms around his

neck and laid her cheek against his silken
warmth.

'I'll never forget you,' she whispered
brokenly.

'You have been a good friend, Gina. I
will not forget you either.' Comet allowed
her to hug him one last time, then gently
backed away. 'Farewell. Ride well and
true,' he said in a deep musical neigh.

There was a final flash of violet light
and a silent explosion of rainbow sparks
that tinkled like fairy laughter as they
touched the grass.

Comet spread his golden wings and
soared upwards. He faded and was gone.

Gina stood there, stunned by how fast
everything had happened. Her throat
ached with unshed tears. Something lay
in the grass. It was a single glittering gold

wing feather. Bending down, she picked it up.

The feather tingled against her hand as it faded to a cream colour. As Gina slipped it into her pocket she knew she would always keep it to remind herself of the magic pony and the amazing adventure they had shared.

She turned sadly, about to walk back up the paddock, and saw Willow waiting at the fence for her. The little chestnut pony reached out and very gently touched her arm. 'I'm still here. We'll look after each other,' she seemed to be saying.

Gina's heart swelled and a smile rose up from deep within her as she knew that Comet had made sure she had a new pony friend for when he left her forever. And with the magic pony's help, she had rediscovered her love of riding.

'Thank you for being my friend, Comet,' she whispered. 'I hope you find Destiny and get back safely to Rainbow Mist Island.'

Out Now

Magic Ponies

Could you be a little pony's special friend?

Magic Ponies

Seaside Summer

SUE BENTLEY

puffin.co.uk

Magic Ponies

A New Friend

A Special Wish

A Twinkle of Hooves

Showjumping Dreams

Seaside Summer

Riding Rescue

Winter Wonderland

Pony Camp

puffin.co.uk

Coming Soon

Magic Reindeer

Could you be a little reindeer's special friend?

Magic Reindeer

A Christmas Wish

SUE BENTLEY

puffin.co.uk

It all started with a Scarecrow

Puffin is well over sixty years old.

Sounds ancient, doesn't it? But Puffin has never been
so lively. We're always on the lookout for the next big
idea, which is how it began all those years ago.

Penguin Books was a big idea from the mind of
a man called Allen Lane, who in 1935 invented
the quality paperback and changed the world.
**And from great Penguins, great Puffins grew,
changing the face of children's books forever.**

The first four Puffin Picture Books were hatched in 1940 and the
first Puffin story book featured a man with broomstick arms called
Worzel Gummidge. In 1967 Kaye Webb, Puffin Editor, started the
Puffin Club, promising to **'make children into readers'.**
She kept that promise and over 200,000 children became
devoted Puffineers through their quarterly installments of
Puffin Post, which is now back for a new generation.

Many years from now, we hope you'll look back and
remember Puffin with a smile. **No matter what your age
or what you're into, there's a Puffin for everyone.**
The possibilities are endless, but one thing is for sure:
whether it's a picture book or a paperback, a sticker book
or a hardback, **if it's got that little Puffin
on it – it's bound to be good.**

Magic Ponies

Win a Magic Ponies goody bag!

Golden feathers from Comet's wings are falling out as he desperately tries to find his twin sister, Destiny, who is still lost in our world! The feathers carry a secret message for Destiny.

Two words from the message can be found in magic golden feathers hidden in *Seaside Summer* and *Riding Rescue*.

To help save Destiny from danger, find the hidden words and put them together to complete the message. Send it in to us and each month we will put every correct message in a draw and pick out one lucky winner to receive a whole stable of Magic Ponies goodies!

Send your secret message, name and address on a postcard to:

Magic Ponies competition

Puffin Books

80 Strand

London WC2R 0RL

Please help Comet save his sister!

Good luck!